THE GHOST AND BERTIE BOGGIN

Bertie Boggin was the smallest
Boggin in a house full of Bogginses.

The Ghost and Bertie Boggin

Written by
MARTIN WADDELL

Illustrated by
TONY ROSS

WALKER BOOKS
AND SUBSIDIARIES
LONDON · BOSTON · SYDNEY

For Bernagh and Bill and Catherine Semple
who believed in the Ghost

First published 1980 by Faber and Faber Ltd
under the name Catherine Sefton

This edition published 2000 by Walker Books Ltd
87 Vauxhall Walk, London SE11 5HJ

2 4 6 8 10 9 7 5 3 1

Text © 1980, 2000 Martin Waddell
Illustrations © 2000 Tony Ross

This book has been typeset in Plantin Light
Printed in England by Clays Ltd, St Ives plc

British Library Cataloguing in Publication Data
A catalogue record for this book
is available from the British Library.

ISBN 0-7445-5944-8

CONTENTS

*The Ghost was sitting on top of the pile of
coal reading yesterday's* Evening Haunt.

BEWARE OF THE GHOST!

Bertie Boggin was the smallest Boggin in a house full of Bogginses. He was smaller than his sister Elsie, smaller than his brother Max, and not quite as big as their dog, Tojo.

One morning the Bogginses decided to play Cannibals.

"I am the Chief Cannibal," said Max. "I go around eating people."

"What people?" asked Elsie.

"Bertie," said Max.

"Oh no," said Bertie.

"Polite dinners don't answer back," said Elsie.

"Ready?" said Max. "Steady…"

Bertie didn't wait for the Eat-The-Bertie game to begin. Like any other worried dinner he went straight to the kitchen, where Mrs Boggin was lying under the sink listening to the pipes and wondering if the cistern was going to explode.

"Are you dead?" Bertie asked, anxiously.

"No," said Mrs Boggin. "Buzz off, Bertie. I am waiting for the house to blow up."

"Max is *not* going to eat me," said Bertie. Then he gave a big sniff, and his eyes went watery.

"Of course he isn't, Bertie," said Mrs Boggin, disengaging herself from the U-pipe and emerging bottom first from under the sink. She wiped his face and made him blow his nose and said, "Nobody is going to eat you, Bertie."

"Yum," said Max, from the doorway. "Yum-yum-yum. I'll have Bertie in my tum!"

"Max," said Mrs Boggin, in her best bloodcurdling voice. "I don't think Eating Bertie is a good game, do you?"

"It was Max's idea," said Elsie. "I knew all along that it was silly."

"You're all big enough now to play together properly," said Mrs Boggin.

"I'm not going to play with them ever again," said Bertie, and he went out to the back yard and sat on the bin.

Max went up to the top bedroom and made Eating Faces at Bertie through the window. Then he got tired of doing that and went away to thump Elsie.

Bertie kicked the side of the bin, which made it rock, like a boat, but Mrs Boggin

9

knocked against the kitchen window-pane with the dish mop and stopped him just before he discovered America.

Bertie got off the bin lid.

No one to play with.

Nothing to do.

And then ...

... he saw ...

... the sign!

It was written on the whitewashed wall of the coalshed in coal-dust letters. It read:

NOTICE
BEWARE OF THE
GHOST

(signed) the ghost

Beneath "(signed) *The Ghost*" there was a

black skull and crossbones, which impressed Bertie very much.

"BEWARE OF THE GHOST" is what the notice said, but Bertie couldn't read it, because he was only in Class P2 at school, and behind with his reading. Instead of bewaring of the Ghost, he put his head around the coalshed door to see if there were any more skulls and crossbones inside.

There had been changes made in the coalshed. Someone had swept the floor with the yard brush. On the shelves were a billy-can and a box labelled "Tea". On the wall opposite the shelf was a picture of a lady holding a lamp.

The Ghost was sitting on top of the pile of coal reading yesterday's *Evening Haunt*. He was studying the Stop Press Deaths when he heard someone gasp. He looked up, and

11

saw Bertie.

"Good morning," said the Ghost politely.

"Who ... who... ?" stuttered Bertie, amazed to find a slightly transparent someone sitting on the coal.

"Florence Nightingale," said the Ghost, thinking that Bertie was talking about the picture. "She was a very great nurse, and a special friend of mine, Bertie."

"How did you know *my* name?" said Bertie.

"You are Bertie Boggin," said the Ghost. "Ghosts have special ways of knowing things."

"*Ghosts!*" gasped Bertie.

Bertie had never seen a ghost before. He blinked his eyes and took a close look at the Ghost, and then he took an even closer look *through* the Ghost.

"I don't *think* I believe in you," said Bertie cautiously.

"I may have fallen on hard times, but there is no need to be insulting," said the Ghost, sounding hurt. "If you don't believe in me, then who do you think you are talking to?"

"Oh," said Bertie, and he sat down on the slack to think about it.

"If you are a ghost," Bertie said, "do something ghostly. Like ... like ... *Goober and the Ghost Chasers.* Do something like that."

"If I must, I must," said the Ghost, patiently ... *and he disappeared!*

Bertie got up from his seat on the slack and climbed to the top of the coal pile, where the Ghost had been.

No sign of the Ghost.

"Are you there?" Bertie asked. "I believe in you *now*. You can appear if you want to. Come on then, appear!"

But the Ghost did not appear.

Bertie was annoyed. Nobody else in P2 of Kitchener Street Primary School had ever seen a ghost, and he had been about to be one-up, until the Ghost disappeared.

"I'm not afraid of you, you know," Bertie said. "You may be able to disappear, but I'm not afraid of you. I'm not afraid of anything. I'm the bravest boy in P2." He said it in what he hoped was a ghost-scaring voice, but he didn't feel brave.

He sat down on the coal where the Ghost had been. It was slightly colder than the rest of the coal, and made him shiver.

"I allow you to appear," he said hopefully.

No Ghost. Bertie began to wonder if he

14

had insulted the Ghost, without meaning to. Perhaps ghosts didn't like being told that they weren't believed in.

And then

C-R-E-A-K!

The door of the coalshed swung open, and Bertie shut his eyes, tightly. But it wasn't the Ghost reappearing, it was Elsie. She put her head around the door and saw Bertie sitting on top of the coal with his eyes shut, looking scared.

"He's in here, Mum," Elsie said. "He's sitting on the coal, and he's all filthy black."

"*Bertie Boggin!*" Mrs Boggin roared, and the next moment Bertie was removed from the coalshed.

There are scrubbings and scrubbings, and the scrubbing Bertie got was a real *scrubbing* scrubbing, the sort he didn't like.

"What possessed you to go in there in your school clothes?" said Mrs Boggin, lunging at Bertie with the flannel. "What were you doing, Bertie?"

"Talking," said Bertie.

"Talking?" said Mrs Boggin. "Who to?"

Bertie looked at her through the eye which wasn't covered by wet flannel. He was usually a truthful person, but he didn't think she was going to believe him.

"To a Ghost," he said.

"What ghost?" said Mrs Boggin scornfully.

She didn't find out what ghost because at that moment Elsie tripped over Max's zobo monster and fell downstairs. She didn't break any bones, but she was carrying a tin of orange paint from the top bedroom at the time, and the tin went up in the air and came down paint first on top of Tojo and the hall

16

carpet. Tojo had a dog's life with the Bogginses.

"Bertie's been seeing ghosts," Elsie reported to Mr Boggin, when he came home from work. "And where do you think Max left his zobo monster?"

"Bertie's ghost was in the coalshed," said Max, quickly, because he didn't want to discuss people being tripped up by zobo monsters. "Bertie got black and Mum had to wash his clothes with him in them and he said he was talking to a ghost, but he wasn't, because there aren't any, are there?"

"Of course not," said Mr Boggin, sniffing to see if he could find out what was for tea.

"Bertie is a little liar," said Max. "I always said he was, but you never believed me."

"*Max*," said Mrs Boggin threateningly.

"Is it bacon, Edna?" asked Mr Boggin.

"And cabbage," said Mrs Boggin. She had made it bacon and cabbage because that was his favourite dinner, and he was going to need a favourite dinner to get over the shock when he heard about the paint in the hall.

"Bertie's a liar," said Max. "You said there are no ghosts, so Bertie's a liar!"

"*Maximillian!*" said Mr Boggin.

"I'm not and there are," said Bertie, but nobody heard him, because he was under the table.

"It was just Bertie's imagination, Max," Mrs Boggin said, but Max didn't hear her. He was watching his father. Mr Boggin had put down his knife and fork and was staring at the strange orange dog which was staring back at him through the yard window.

"That's … that's…" Mr Boggin stuttered, because the dog certainly looked familiar, although it was the wrong colour.

"That's our Tojo," said Mrs Boggin.

"Short for Thomas Joseph," said Bertie helpfully.

"I am afraid there has been a little accident, dear," said Mrs Boggin. Then everybody stopped talking until Mr Boggin had examined the large orange paint stain in the hall, which had a dog-shaped patch in the middle of it. Mr Boggin had walked into the house without noticing it, but as soon as it was pointed out to him he made up for lost time.

"Bertie," said Mrs Boggin, when she was putting him to bed. "Bertie, what were you doing in the coalshed before the paint was spilt?"

Bertie told her for the second time that day.

19

Mrs Boggin tried to look very serious, because she took being a mother very seriously. "That ghost is one of your imaginings, Bertie," she said, in her best gentle-but-firm voice. "I am your mother. I don't mind if you have a pretend ghost, so long as you and I know that it is just pretend, and you don't go pestering other people with it."

"I'm not pretending," said Bertie.

"There are no such things as ghosts," said Mrs Boggin. "So you must be pretending, mustn't you?"

"Y-e-s," said Bertie, doubtfully. "Only ... only ... I wish he was real."

Mrs Boggin looked surprised.

"If he was real, I would have someone to play with when I'm not at school," said Bertie.

He lay in bed thinking about it, after his mother had gone downstairs. She was right, of course.

"I know there are no ghosts, so she must be right," Bertie muttered, lying in the darkness with the blankets pulled up to his chin.

And then ...

　　... there was a rustle ...

　　　　... and something like a gasp...

　　　　　　... and the Ghost came floating down the chimney and settled on the mantelpiece, where he made a ghost-shaped sooty mark.

"Good evening," said the Ghost.

"I *knew* you were real," said Bertie, opening one eye carefully to look at the Ghost. Then he opened the other one, and sat up.

"And I knew you were real too, Bertie," said the Ghost, seeing it from his own ghostly point of view.

"They don't believe in you downstairs," said Bertie, beginning to get confused again. "Max says I'm a liar and Dad doesn't believe in ghosts and my Mother says you're pretend and I can't see you because you aren't real. But you are real." He stopped to consider the problem. "I expect ... I expect they can't see you because they don't believe in ghosts."

"I expect so," said the Ghost.

"I believe in ghosts," said Bertie quickly, in case the Ghost should be insulted, and start disappearing again.

"I have to believe in ghosts, because I am one," said the Ghost, crossing his legs and settling back on the mantelpiece.

"You'll be my friend, won't you?" said Bertie, anxiously.

"Oh yes, of course I will," said the Ghost. "It is a long time since I had someone to be friends with."

"Good," said Bertie, and he snuggled down in bed, feeling happy.

"Ghost," said Bertie. "We'll be Best Friends, won't we?"

"Best Friends," said the Ghost. "*Yes*. I like the sound of that. We'll be Best Friends, Bertie."

Bertie went to sleep, and the Ghost curled up on the mantelpiece and lay there glowing softly until midnight came, when it was time to put on his coat and go out haunting again.

"BRANDYBALLS!" exclaimed Mrs Boggin…
"Bertie, how did these get into my trolley?"

THE GHOST GOES SHOPPING

One afternoon, when Max and Elsie were in the front room doing their homework, Mrs Boggin said, "Put on your red jumper, Bertie. We are going shopping."

Bertie went to his chest of drawers to get the red jumper and found the Ghost curled up inside the jumper drawer taking a well-earned rest after a hard night's haunting at the Spectre's Arms in Culloden Street.

"Wake up, Ghost," said Bertie. "You are sleeping on my red jumper and I need it. I am going shopping."

The Ghost floated out of the drawer and stretched himself to full everyday ghost size.

"Your drawer is a little too small for comfort," he said, uncrumpling himself in front of the mirror.

"I like shopping," said Bertie.

The Ghost didn't hear him. The Ghost had gone back to the jumper drawer and was searching frantically inside it. "Where is my hat?" he asked, in an anxious voice. Sometimes when the Ghost came home late from the Spectre's Arms he left things behind him, and he didn't want to lose his hat.

"Your hat is under Max's bed, and it is very dusty," said Bertie. Mrs Boggin wouldn't let Bertie throw clothes under beds because she said she was fed up wearing her knees to the bone crawling around on the floor to fetch them. "What do you want your hat for?"

"To put on my head," said the Ghost, wisping in beneath Max's bed to fetch his hat, which had somehow become entangled with a model of Nelson's *Victory* complete with plastic cannon.

"Your head will get dusty," said Bertie.

"Ghosts are used to the odd cobweb, although we draw the line at spiders," said the Ghost. "However, I will dust my hat before putting it on my head. I must look smart today."

"Why?" asked Bertie.

"Ghosts like to look smart, going shopping," said the Ghost.

"But nobody can see you, except me," Bertie pointed out.

"I can see me, and I am not Nobody," said the Ghost, with dignity, and then he went up the chimney and down the drainpipe to the coalshed to fetch his best coat and boots.

Mrs Boggin and Bertie and the Ghost and his hat went to the Ormeau Road and caught a bus. They sat on the top deck so that Bertie could look out at all the people.

"This is a nice bus," said the Ghost to Bertie. "Ghosts do not usually like buses."

"Why not?" said Bertie.

"People sit on ghosts' hats in buses," said the Ghost.

"But you are wearing your hat," objected Bertie.

"That is what I mean," said the Ghost. "People sit on ghosts' hats whilst ghosts are wearing them. It can be very uncomfortable to be a ghost on a crowded bus, I can tell you. I like *this* bus because there aren't many people on it to sit on me."

"Except me," said Bertie, "and I wouldn't."

They got off the bus and went into the Forestside shopping centre. Mrs Boggin selected a wheel-around trolley.

"Me in the trolley seat!" said Bertie.

"No, Bertie," said Mrs Boggin. "You are much too big. Schoolboys do not go in trolley seats."

"Ghosts like trolley seats," said the Ghost, settling himself comfortably for a ride around the shelves.

"I should have left you at home," grumbled Bertie.

Mrs Boggin had the whole week's shopping to do. Cornflakes and porridge and baked beans and orange squash and frozen peas and celery and bananas and hair curlers and razor blades and...

"Sweeties," said Bertie, looking up at the shelves.

But Mrs Boggin didn't hear him. She was busy fussing over tomatoes and potatoes and rice and white flour and dog food and elastic bands and Special Offer Soap Powder (twenty pence off) and three blue dishes and marzipan and jelly shapes.

The Ghost was inspecting a stand full of paperback books. "Ghosts like books," he explained, looking down on Bertie from his seat in the trolley. "There are exciting stories in books about people ghosts used to know."

"I want sweeties," said Bertie, who was in no mood for bookworm conversations with a ghost.

"What sort of sweeties do you want, Bertie?" asked the Ghost.

"Brandyballs," said Bertie, loudly, in the hope that his mother would hear.

"Bertie wants brandyballs, Edna," the

Ghost said. He was speaking to Mrs Boggin. Her name *was* Edna, but she didn't hear him, because she didn't believe in ghosts.

"Don't fuss me, Bertie," Mrs Boggin said, picking up bacon and sausages and shiny tinfoil and dog meal and asparagus tips and four blue ball-point pens and a cabbage and a cheese grater, but not a single brandyball.

"I *like* brandyballs," said Bertie.

"Bertie *likes* brandyballs, Edna," said the Ghost.

But Mrs Boggin didn't hear either of them.

"I *want* brandyballs," said Bertie.

"Bertie *wants* brandyballs," echoed the Ghost, not very hopefully.

Mrs Boggin paid no attention, and so the Ghost decided to do something about it. After all, Bertie was his Best Friend.

31

They went to the check-out, and the lady took all Mrs Boggin's purchases out of the trolley.

There was porridge and cornflakes and baked beans and orange squash and frozen peas and brandyballs and celery and bananas and hair curlers and razor blades and *brandyballs* and tomatoes and potatoes and rice and white flour and dog food and BRANDYBALLS and elastic bands and Special Offer Soap Powder (twenty pence off) and three blue dishes and marzipan and jelly shapes and...

"BRANDYBALLS!" exclaimed Mrs Boggin, snatching the bag of brandyballs off the counter. "Bertie, how did these get into my trolley?"

"I don't know," said Bertie. "It must have been the Ghost."

"Then the Ghost can put them all back," said Mrs Boggin, storming round to the brandyball shelf.

She looked at the shelf.

She looked at Bertie.

Bertie was small for a P2, and the sweet stand was tall. There were lots of sweets on the bottom, of course, but the brandyball shelf was high up.

She looked up at the shelf and down at Bertie, *up* at the shelf and *down* at Bertie again, and then she went pale.

Bertie was too small to reach the brandyball shelf. Someone standing up in the trolley basket might have managed it, but not Bertie. Bertie had his feet firmly on the ground.

"Brandy!" said Mrs Boggin, faintly.

"That's a splendid idea, Edna," said the

Ghost, who was very fond of a little brandy after hours in the Spectre's Arms.

"They're brandy*balls*," said Bertie. "Couldn't I have just one packet, Mum?"

"Y ... e ... s, dear," said Mrs Boggin, in a shaky voice, and she handed Bertie three packets.

They waited outside for Mr Boggin and the others to pick them up in the Bogginses' Mini, and they drove home in silence. When they got back to Livermore Street Bertie went to the coalshed to share his brandyballs with his Best Friend, and Mrs Boggin and Mr Boggin had a serious talk in the front room, with the door closed.

"Bertie's Ghost, Edna?" said Mr Boggin, in amazement.

"Bertie's Ghost," said Mrs Boggin.

"There is no ghost, Edna," said Mr

34

Ghost, who was very fond of a little brandy after hours in the Spectre's Arms.

"They're brandy*balls*," said Bertie. "Couldn't I have just one packet, Mum?"

"Y ... e ... s, dear," said Mrs Boggin, in a shaky voice, and she handed Bertie three packets.

They waited outside for Mr Boggin and the others to pick them up in the Bogginses' Mini, and they drove home in silence. When they got back to Livermore Street Bertie went to the coalshed to share his brandyballs with his Best Friend, and Mrs Boggin and Mr Boggin had a serious talk in the front room, with the door closed.

"Bertie's Ghost, Edna?" said Mr Boggin, in amazement.

"Bertie's Ghost," said Mrs Boggin.

"There is no ghost, Edna," said Mr

Ghost said. He was speaking to Mrs Boggin. Her name *was* Edna, but she didn't hear him, because she didn't believe in ghosts.

"Don't fuss me, Bertie," Mrs Boggin said, picking up bacon and sausages and shiny tinfoil and dog meal and asparagus tips and four blue ball-point pens and a cabbage and a cheese grater, but not a single brandyball.

"I *like* brandyballs," said Bertie.

"Bertie *likes* brandyballs, Edna," said the Ghost.

But Mrs Boggin didn't hear either of them.

"I *want* brandyballs," said Bertie.

"Bertie *wants* brandyballs," echoed the Ghost, not very hopefully.

Mrs Boggin paid no attention, and so the Ghost decided to do something about it. After all, Bertie was his Best Friend.

They went to the check-out, and the lady took all Mrs Boggin's purchases out of the trolley.

There was porridge and cornflakes and baked beans and orange squash and frozen peas and brandyballs and celery and bananas and hair curlers and razor blades and *brandyballs* and tomatoes and potatoes and rice and white flour and dog food and BRANDYBALLS and elastic bands and Special Offer Soap Powder (twenty pence off) and three blue dishes and marzipan and jelly shapes and…

"BRANDYBALLS!" exclaimed Mrs Boggin, snatching the bag of brandyballs off the counter. "Bertie, how did these get into my trolley?"

"I don't know," said Bertie. "It must have been the Ghost."

"Then the Ghost can put them all back," said Mrs Boggin, storming round to the brandyball shelf.

She looked at the shelf.

She looked at Bertie.

Bertie was small for a P2, and the sweet stand was tall. There were lots of sweets on the bottom, of course, but the brandyball shelf was high up.

She looked up at the shelf and down Bertie, *up* at the shelf and *down* at Be again, and then she went pale.

Bertie was too small to reach brandyball shelf. Someone standing the trolley basket might have managed not Bertie. Bertie had his feet firmly ground.

"Brandy!" said Mrs Boggin, fair

"That's a splendid idea, Edna

Boggin, sternly. "I've never heard such nonsense. Bertie is making him up, because he has no one of his own age to play with when he isn't at school."

"But..." began Mrs Boggin.

"I don't believe in ghosts, and that's that," said Mr Boggin, scornfully.

"Neither do I," said Mrs Boggin. "Of course not. It's absolute nonsense, isn't it?"

"Absolutely," said Mr Boggin, but he couldn't explain the Mystery of the Brandyballs.

"Ghost picnics are nice," said Bertie.

THE GHOST'S PICNIC

It was the morning of the Kitchener Street Primary School Special Picnic for Senior Boys and Girls.

Elsie and Max got up early and made so much noise banging around the house that they wakened Bertie and disturbed the Ghost in the middle of a pleasant dream about Florence Nightingale.

"We're on our way to Millisle!" hummed Elsie, rolling up her swimsuit in a towel.

"Oh we do like to be beside the seaside. We do like to be beside the sea," sang Max, picking up a bucket and spade which he had fortunately found hidden under the stairs.

"That is my bucket and spade," said Bertie, from his bed. "But I allow you to borrow it."

"Thanks a lot," said Max gruffly, and he went off down the stairs chanting, "We *do* like to be beside the sea…" at the top of his voice.

"I want to go on the Special Picnic to Millisle," Bertie said to the Ghost, who had abandoned Florence Nightingale and was sitting cross-legged in front of the electric fire, hoping that someone would switch it on. It was a dull mizzly day, and the Ghost had decided that he was staying in the house with Bertie, in the hope of keeping warm. Ghosts are cold enough to begin with, without the weather helping.

38

"Picnics are all very well," said the Ghost. "Ghosts prefer hot toast in front of the fire."

Bertie wasn't listening to him. Bertie was getting out of bed.

"I don't see why I shouldn't go on the Special Picnic to Millisle," he said. "I bet I'd be a better picnicker than Max," and he went off downstairs to tell his mother about it.

"What are you doing downstairs in your pyjamas?" said Mrs Boggin, when Bertie appeared in the kitchen. "And no slippers! You'll catch your death of cold! Go upstairs and get dressed at once!"

"But…" began Bertie.

"At once," said Mrs Boggin. She was busy looking for Max's raincoat, in case the day turned wet. Max had been using it as a Bat-Boggin cloak for jumping downstairs, and couldn't remember where it was.

Bertie went upstairs, put on his clothes, and came down again carrying his bathing suit and a towel from the bathroom. "I am going to go on the Special Picnic to Millisle with Elsie and Max," he announced.

"You're only a P2," said Max, scornfully. "The Special Picnic at Millisle is Seniors only."

"Not titches," said Elsie, who was cross about having to wear her waterproof hat to the picnic, because it was bright yellow and made her look like a fat parrot.

"Not this year, Bertie," said Mrs Boggin.

Bertie looked angry and maybe-about-to-cry.

"He's going to cry," said Max.

"No I'm not," said Bertie.

"You'll go on the picnic when you are bigger, Bertie," said Mrs Boggin. "I'm

Elsie and Max Boggin left the Bogginses' house in Livermore Street at half-past nine. At ten o'clock it started to rain heavily. It rained on them all the way to Millisle, all through the picnic, all the way round the lighthouse at Donaghadee, and all the way back again. They arrived home at half-past five and came squelching into the hall.

"Hot soup. Bed," ordered Mrs Boggin, wringing out Elsie.

"I want to stay up and ... a ... a ... a ... tishoo!" said Max, as a deep puddle formed around his feet. He was a very wet Bat-Boggin indeed.

"Bed," said Mrs Boggin, and she bundled Elsie and Max off up the stairs, although it was long before their bed-time.

She made them hot tomato soup. Then she looked around for something special to cheer them up.

She couldn't find the strawberry jam.

The chocolate éclairs were missing from the Quality Street Box where they lived.

There was no toffee in the Toffee Tin.

The green jelly had been scraped out of the jelly dish, by some Boggin unknown.

Someone had taken the last two apples and the bottle of lemonade that lived in the kitchen cupboard.

"Ghost picnics are nice," said Bertie, the only child Boggin left standing, who had gone out to the coalshed to talk to the Ghost. "But I still don't understand *why* we had to have your ghost picnic in the coalshed, where it is difficult to see what we are eating."

"Ghosts can see in the dark," said the Ghost, licking the last of the chocolate éclair off his ghostly fingers. "People can't. That means that ghosts get most of the food. That is why ghosts have their picnics in the dark."

"Oh," said Bertie.

"You can't complain," said the Ghost. "You have eaten five éclairs!"

"Four," said Bertie.

"*Five*," said the Ghost. "I may have wispy fingers, but I can still count on them. Five éclairs, and a lot more besides. And you didn't get soaked to the skin and sent to bed. You had your picnic in a nice dry coalshed. You didn't have to eat wet banana sandwiches in a bus shelter in Millisle like Elsie and Max. You had a Special In-The-Dark Ghost Picnic, because you are my Best Friend."

"Am I?" said Bertie, sounding very pleased.

"My *specially* Best Friend," said the Ghost.

"Oh dear, oh dear!" panted the Ghost,
settling on the highest branch he could reach.

Tojo and the Ghost

"Grrr! Rrrrfffff! Whhhhhhaaarrrrfffffufuf! Grrra-amble!"

"What's the matter with that dog?" grumbled Mr Boggin, who was trying to read the *Sunday Times* and do the dishes at the same time, because Mrs Boggin was on strike. She had gone to visit Aunt Amanda in Ballynahinch, leaving the rest of the Bogginses behind her to enjoy the first weekend of the school holidays.

"Grrr! Rrrrffufufuf!" Tojo bounded up and down the back yard by the coalshed, barking at something.

"He's chasing his tail," said Elsie. "Silly dog." She was trying to scrape burnt baked beans out of the smallest saucepan, and she wasn't enjoying doing it.

At that moment Bertie came rocketing down the stairs and crashed through the living room, heading for the back yard.

"Bertie!" Mr Boggin thundered, as the kitchen door slammed.

"Grrr! Whaaarrrruuufff!"

The Ghost sat on the roof of the coalshed, trying to look dignified and historical, but feeling very cross inside his ghostly skin.

"Ghosts," he said to Bertie, "do not like being snuffed and barked at by large hairy dogs. Ghosts have had a hard life and a long one. This particular Ghost has moved out of the Spectre's Arms and into your coalshed in

48

order to obtain a little peace and quiet away from the Haunted Cellar Disco."

"I'm terribly sorry, Ghost," said Bertie, and he caught Tojo by the collar and pulled him away from the coalshed. Bertie was afraid that the Ghost would decide to disappear again, right at the beginning of the holidays.

"Grrrrrr!" growled Tojo.

"In you go," said Bertie, and he pushed Tojo into the kitchen, where Tojo tripped Mr Boggin and made him drop the dish mop into the teapot, which fell off the table on to Max's foot. Max jumped and hit his head on the cupboard door, which swung back and banged into the cornflakes, which fell over into the dog's dish, where Tojo ate them.

When Tojo had finished eating cornflakes

he went into the living room and climbed up on the sofa to look out at the back yard.

Tojo was worried about the back yard.

Tojo was a good dog. He knew his job. He was supposed to eat things, take people for walks, and guard the house.

It was guarding the house that was worrying him.

Tojo hadn't seen anything, but he had *sniffed*. And what he had sniffed wasn't burglars or people with bones for dogs or foolish fearless cats. What he had sniffed was something distinctly ghost-like, but snuffle and bark as he might he couldn't find out what it was.

"I suppose having a Ghost in the coalshed is confusing for a dog who isn't very bright," said Bertie, who sometimes found it confusing himself.

"Having a not very bright dog in the back yard is even more confusing for a Ghost of superior intelligence," said the Ghost, immodestly. "There I was, dreaming of Florence Nightingale, and days gone by, and penny tram-rides from the Junction, when out bounced that dog!"

"You should try to make friends with Tojo," Bertie suggested.

"Ghosts are naturally friendly, but not with dogs who snuffle them!" said the Ghost.

"You could take Tojo for walks. He likes that. That would make him like you."

"Hmmmph," said the Ghost. "Do you think so?"

"Yes," said Bertie.

And so, at half-past two when Mr Boggin and Bertie took Tojo for his run in Ormeau

Park, the Ghost put on his best coat and boots and came with them.

They were half-way across the park when Tojo got his first whiff of ghost.

"Grrrr! Wharraavuuff!" Tojo dashed past Bertie, his tail wagging and his big feet pounding the ground. The Ghost took one look at the large hairy thing that was crashing towards him and set off for the trees. He had seen nothing like it since the Charge of the Light Brigade.

"Tojo!" cried Bertie.

"Grrrrrr!"

The Ghost arrived puffing and blowing at the foot of the nearest tree and quickly climbed up out of harm's way. Tojo arrived at the bottom, bouncing and prancing and barking fit to burst.

"Oh dear, oh dear!" panted the Ghost,

settling on the highest branch he could reach.

"Why is Tojo attacking that tree?" asked Mr Boggin, who had settled on a park bench to read the part of his Sunday paper which had *not* dropped into the washing-up liquid.

"It is because he's chasing the Gho…" Bertie started to explain, but then he stopped. Mrs Boggin was prepared to listen to Bertie's stories about the Ghost, but Mr Boggin was not. "*Ghosts are nonsense,*" Mr Boggin said. "*I don't want to hear any of that talk in this house.*" Mr Boggin didn't believe in ghosts, of course. Bertie was the only Boggin who believed in ghosts, and the only Boggin who could see that there was one in the coalshed. Instead of talking about the Ghost, Bertie said, "What sort of dog is that, Dad?", hoping that the change of subject would keep him out of trouble.

"That" was a big dog, about twice the size of Tojo, and three times as fierce-looking. It had heard the commotion when Tojo set off to chase the Ghost, and had run across the park to see if there were any good fights going on.

"SSSSnnnnrrrr!" snarled the big dog, who was heavyweight champion of the Ormeau Road, and the next moment it jumped on top of poor Tojo and tried to bite off his ears.

"Tojo!" cried Bertie, and Mr Boggin started to run, yelling and waving his rolled-up paper at the big dog.

But somebody else came to the rescue first, just when Tojo looked like becoming a dog's dinner.

"Yaaarrpp!" went the big dog, in fright, as something ghost-like and very brave came crashing down on its head, and started pulling its ears.

"*YAAAPUPUPUP! AAAPPUP!*" choked the big dog, as the ghost-like something punched it hard on the nose.

"Yee-lllpupup!" howled the big dog as the ghost-like something caught it by the tail, twisted and twirled.

"YeeePUUP!" yelped the big dog, and it scrambled away from Tojo as fast as it could, and fled across the park with its tail between its legs.

"I don't understand," said Mr Boggin, scratching his head in bewilderment. "Did our Tojo do that?"

Tojo was standing at the foot of the tree wagging his tail in a very friendly way, and licking someone Mr Boggin couldn't see, someone who was feeling rather proud of his ghostly self now that the battle was over.

"If I hadn't seen Tojo do it with my own eyes…" Mr Boggin shook his head in bewilderment.

They all went home.

"You were brave, Ghost," said Bertie admiringly.

"It was nothing," said the Ghost. "Remind me to tell you about the Battle of Inkerman some time, will you? Now that *was* a fight, and no mistake." And he settled down on the slack with his new ally Tojo, and his old friend Bertie Boggin, and told them all about Florence Nightingale and Inkerman and Balaclava and the Charge of the Light Brigade and what-Lord-Raglan-said. Bertie didn't interrupt him, although he had heard it all before.

"There is something *odd* about this house,

these days," said Mr Boggin to Mrs Boggin, when she came in off the late bus from Ballynahinch. He wanted to tell her about Tojo, but after she had seen the mess in the kitchen he wasn't able to tell her anything.

When Mrs Boggin went to bed she looked in on Bertie and Max and Elsie on the way up. They were all fast asleep, so fast asleep that one of them was snoring.

"One of the children is snoring," she told Mr Boggin when she reached the bedroom.

"No they're not," said Mr Boggin. "I can't hear a thing."

"Well, I can," said Mrs Boggin. "It must be Bertie's friend the Ghost!"

She was right, of course, although she didn't know it. She was right, but the odd thing was that she heard anything at all, for Mrs Boggin still *said* that she didn't believe in ghosts.

"Poor me! Poor me! I am a very sick Ghost."

SPOTTED GHOST

One day Max Boggin came home from the Playscheme in Ormeau Park with a bad cold. The following morning it was much worse and Max had to stay in bed and miss the five-a-side football and an excursion. The *next* morning when Max woke up he didn't look like Max.

"Max's eyes are all red and he's grotty-spotty!" reported Elsie, who had looked in on Max on her way downstairs in order to tell him about the baseball he would be missing. Elsie liked telling Max about things he would be missing.

"My eyes hurt something rotten!" said Max, in a weak voice.

"Measles!" said Mrs Boggin. She went straight downstairs and rang for Doctor Gibson.

"Lovely measles!" said Elsie. "Max looks awful with measles. I mean much *awfuller* than usual. If we're lucky, maybe he'll stay like that for ever." Then she thought of a poem and went up to say it to Max.

Old Ugly Spotty Head
Has to spend his life in bed.

And then she added gleefully: "I'm a poet, and I don't know it."

And then she coughed.

And then she coughed again, and scratched the spot on her cheek.

One of the spots on her cheek. One that

matched the other ones, which suddenly seemed to be appearing all over her.

"Serves you right," said Max, with some satisfaction.

"Elsie, bed!" said Mrs Boggin, and Elsie had to go to bed too.

"Both measled," announced Doctor Gibson. "Stay in bed, follow the treatment, watch the temperature, no excitement, keep them out of bright light."

Elsie grew some lovely spots, and became proud of them. She had more spots than Max. She knew because she counted them.

Aunt Amanda Boggin came up from Ballynahinch on the bus with a bag of grapes and a pile of comics. Aunt Amanda read to Elsie and Max, and Mrs Boggin brought them drinks and fresh fruit. Max had oranges and Elsie had bananas and apples, because she didn't like oranges. She was afraid she might swallow the pips. The curtains were kept tightly closed and the only light in the room was a red bulb, which glowed gently in one corner, beside the Manchester United poster.

Bertie wasn't allowed in. He had to sleep in Elsie's room and feed her goldfish.

Bertie tried sitting on the stairs outside the sickroom, but he couldn't hear Aunt Amanda's stories, and nobody brought him drinks and oranges, with or without the pips.

"Ecough! Ecough!" Bertie came into the kitchen, coughing hopefully.

"Don't bother me, Bertie," said Mrs Boggin, who was sitting on the kitchen stool reading about measles in the Medical Dictionary and worrying about Possible Complications.

"I'm coughing," said Bertie. "I think I might have measles, like Max and Elsie."

Mrs Boggin put down the dictionary and looked at him carefully. "No you haven't," she said, in a not-to-be-argued-with-voice. "Not yet, anyway, thank your lucky stars."

"I don't mind having measles," Bertie said.

"Uhuh," muttered Mrs Boggin, trying to find the place where she had stopped reading. "Buzz off, little Bertie."

"I *might* get them, mightn't I?" said Bertie. "Then I'd get spots and grapes and a red light and lots of stories from Aunt Amanda, wouldn't I?"

"You'll get boiled in oil if you don't clear off and leave me in peace," said Mrs Boggin bitterly. "You haven't got measles. You don't want measles. Nobody does. So clear off. Scoot!"

Bertie went out to the coalshed, and Mrs Boggin went upstairs with a tray of soft drinks for the patients and something a little stronger for Aunt Amanda Boggin from Ballynahinch.

"Good morning, Ghost," said Bertie.

"Ooooaaah. Oooooooh," moaned the Ghost.

"Are you having a practice haunt?" said Bertie. He was used to the Ghost doing his Haunting Scales in the coalshed. Haunting is a tricky thing, and trickier still when someone puts a Discotheque in your Haunted Cellar. Sometimes it was the most the Ghost could do to make his groans heard above the music, and a ghost who doesn't keep his groan up isn't worthy of his chains.

"Ooooooh! Aaaaah!" moaned the Ghost. "Poor me! Poor me! I am a very sick Ghost. Go away, Bertie, you might catch it."

"Might I?" said Bertie hopefully, and he peered inside the coalshed.

The Ghost was lying curled up on the slack. His face was covered in spots, and he hadn't felt so awful since the morning after Coronation Day, 1910, when he had thoroughly disgraced himself and fallen in a fountain in Trafalgar Square.

"Measles," said Bertie, and he trotted off to the kitchen. Bertie knew *exactly* what to do when someone had measles.

"Bertie?" said Mrs Boggin. "Bertie, where are you?"

She looked in the front room, to see if he was watching television, but he wasn't. She looked under the stairs in Bat-Boggin's cave, in case Bertie was trespassing there whilst Bat-Boggin lay upstairs being sick, but he wasn't. Then she went out to the back yard.

Humpty Dumpty sat on a wall
Humpty Dumpty had a great fall
All the King's horses and all the King's men
Couldn't put Humpty together again.

She could hear Bertie's voice, but she didn't know where he was at first, although she should have guessed.

"Shall I say Humpty Dumpty again?" Bertie asked brightly, as he offered the Ghost another slice of apple.

"No, no," said the Ghost hastily. "It was very enjoyable *the first time*, but I think I know the story by now, thank you." He was bitterly regretting the Good Old Days, and particularly Florence Nightingale.

"I don't know any other rhymes," said Bertie. "Not right through, anyway."

The door opened.

Mrs Boggin saw Bertie, and the apples, and the oranges, and the fresh fruit drinks and the spare grapes borrowed from Aunt Amanda's bundle, but she didn't see the Ghost.

"BERTIE BOGGIN!" said Mrs Boggin.

"It's for the Ghost," said Bertie. "The Ghost has measles. He is sick. I've been telling him Humpty Dumpty to cheer him up."

"IN THE HOUSE NOW, BERTIE BOGGIN!" thundered Mrs Boggin, grabbing her son.

The door banged shut behind them and the Ghost settled back on the slack. He felt like Humpty Dumpty after the fall, and all he wanted to do was sleep.

The Ghost had a bad day, and by evening he had made up his mind that he would have to do without going to the Spectre's Arms. He managed a little soup and some bread, and the next morning he was well enough to manage a practice clank or two. Afterwards, he made his way slowly up the drainpipe and carefully down the chimney into Bertie's room.

"Spots," said Bertie proudly.

He was sitting up in bed, all covered in spots. Beside him was a large bowl of fruit, and a jug containing fresh orange juice. Mrs Boggin had removed Elsie's goldfish, in case measles were catching.

"Mine are better spots than Max's," said Bertie. "And I've got more than Elsie, whatever she says. She may be in P6, but she can't count for butternuts. I have the best spots of all. And Aunt Amanda Boggin is coming up specially from Ballynahinch to tell me stories."

"Good," said the Ghost, who liked being told stories. The Ghost settled down on the mantelpiece and they compared spots and waited for Aunt Amanda.

"Now, Bertie," said Aunt Amanda. "What do you want me to read to you?"

"Humpty Dumpty," said Bertie happily, and the Ghost sighed, and shimmered a bit, and took another of Aunt Amanda's grapes.

He didn't mind hearing the Humpty Dumpty book, but he *had* heard it all before.

The Ghost was still sitting in the Ghost Train
carriage, looking very pale and frightened,
with his eyes tight shut.

THE GHOST TRAIN

One day, when the Bogginses had finished having measles, Mr Boggin said: "Everybody up and out! We are getting into the Mini and going off for a day at the seaside."

"Dad and Mum and Bertie and Max and me," said Elsie happily.

"And the Ghost," said Bertie.

"No ghost, Bertie," said Mrs Boggin firmly. "I've told you about these ghost stories before, haven't I? Don't bother your father."

"I know you've told me," said Bertie. "But the Ghost is my friend. He's got to come. Otherwise I'll have no one to play with."

"Max and Elsie are your friends," said Mrs Boggin, not very hopefully.

"We're not," said Max.

"He's a little lump!" said Elsie.

"Children!" said Mrs Boggin.

"That's enough," said Mr Boggin firmly. "We're all going to have a happy day at the seaside and enjoy ourselves and Max and Elsie aren't going to tease Bertie, and Bertie isn't going to start any of his ghost nonsense, are you, Bertie?"

Mr Boggin had just stopped talking when he felt someone tickling the back of his neck. At least, he was sure someone was tickling the back of his neck, but when he turned round to see who it was, there was no one there.

"Who...?" he said.

"Who what, Dad?" said Max.

Mr Boggin looked at him, hard. But it couldn't have been Max, because Max was standing in front of him. So was Elsie, and Bertie, and Mrs Boggin didn't go in for tickling, much.

"I ... er ... yes," said Mr Boggin gruffly. And then he spoke very loudly, just to demonstrate to himself that he wasn't the sort of person who imagines himself being tickled. "I want it plainly understood that there will be no ghosts on this trip, Bertie. Right?"

"Except me," said the Ghost, but no one heard him except Bertie, and Bertie kept quiet about it.

Off went the Bogginses' Mini to the seaside, complete with Bogginses and Ghost.

They got to the seaside and went down to the beach. They unpacked the bathing costumes and the rug and the folding table and Mrs Boggin's knitting and Max's cricket bat and the baskets of food and the lemonade and the Lilo and Mr Boggin's book and the coal-bucket.

"Who packed the coal-bucket?" demanded Mr Boggin, wiping coal-dust off his Radio One T-shirt.

"The same person who packed the coal-shovel," said Max, waving it round his head, and almost cutting Elsie's ear off.

"Stop it, Max," said Mrs Boggin.

"Who packed the coal things?" demanded Mr Boggin.

Everybody looked at Bertie.

"It wasn't me," said Bertie, who knew quite well who it was, but wasn't allowed to talk about ghosts.

"I know who I think it was," said Mr Boggin darkly, but he didn't want to spoil the day out, and so he lay down on the Lilo and gave directions to Mrs Boggin about getting the picnic ready, whilst he read his book.

"You could have borrowed my bucket and spade, Ghost," said Bertie, when they went down to paddle.

"I'm an independent-minded Ghost," said the Ghost, who had plans for building a very big castle indeed, and didn't think much of Bertie's plastic spade, which was on the small side.

They stood looking at the water.

"It looks very cold," said Bertie. "I don't think I will paddle just yet."

"Very wise, Bertie," said the Ghost. "I

75

prefer to stay on dry land myself. It is because of jellyfish."

"What about jellyfish?"

"Jellyfish are like ghosts. They float about, and you can see through them, and you can't hear them coming. In fact, some jellyfish think that ghosts are jellyfish and when they see ghosts paddling they try to make friends. Ghosts don't like shaking hands with jellyfish."

"Jellyfish haven't got hands," said Bertie.

"What they have got is much worse to shake hands with," said the Ghost.

Then they started castle-building.

"What a big castle, Bertie!" Mrs Boggin exclaimed in surprise, when she came to call them back for the picnic.

"It's a rotten castle," said Max.

"Twice as big as yours!" said Elsie.

So Max threw sand at Elsie, and Elsie hit him with a dead crab.

"My castle was best, wasn't it?" said Bertie cheerfully, as Mrs Boggin marched them back up the beach.

"*Our* castle," said the Ghost.

"I built the best castle, and I wasn't fighting," Bertie announced to his father. "Max built a rotten castle, and Elsie hit him with her dead crab."

Mr Boggin sat up sleepily, and put his elbow in the ice cream.

"Who put that there?" he said.

"I did," said Mrs Boggin, who wasn't very pleased with anyone, especially husbands who stayed on Lilos reading books while she did the picnic-laying and refereed sand-and-dead-crab boxing matches.

It was a good picnic. Mrs Boggin was

good at picnic food. There were ham sandwiches and peas in the pod and apples and oranges and chocolate fingers and little sausages ... three of Max's disappeared just after he counted them ... and chocolate wafers and tomatoes and lettuce and crusty bread.

"Now," said Mr Boggin, "you tidy up all the things into the car, Edna. I'm taking the children to the fun fair."

"No you're not!" said Mrs Boggin. "I'll take them to the fun fair. You can tidy up!" and off they went.

It was a big fun fair.

They went on the helter-skelter and the dodgems and steera-boats and the roundabout, and Max was sick.

Then Bertie and Elsie went on Little Monte Carlo and the Wall of Death and the

Hall of Mirrors and the Crazy Castle and Bargum's Big Watershoot, and Elsie fell in.

"I want to go home," wailed Elsie.

"My tummy's funny," said Max.

"Bertie!" said Mrs Boggin, looking round for him.

"I don't want to go home," said Bertie, who knew what was coming next. "I'm not sick or wet. I'm having the best time ever."

Mrs Boggin looked at him. He was covered in candyfloss, from one ear to the other. He had torn the knee of his trousers on the helter-skelter, and won a plastic gun at hoop-la. He was very happy-looking, and Mrs Boggin didn't want to disappoint him.

"Let's go home, Mum," wailed Elsie.

"One more ride, Bertie," said Mrs Boggin. "Hurry up now. I'll take Elsie to the Ladies and wring her out. Max will look after you, won't you, Max?"

And off she went.

"What are you going on then, you rotten little lump?" said Max, who was looking very green and pale.

"I know!" said Bertie. "I know, I know!" and off he bounced.

"Max?" said Mrs Boggin, when she came out of the Ladies. "Max? Where's Bertie?"

Max sniffed. "Ghost Train," he said.

"Oh," said Mrs Boggin. "Oh dear! He'll be scared stiff."

"I know," said Max, who hoped Bertie would be.

"You're a little horror, Max," said Mrs Boggin, and she set off with the sniffly Elsie behind her to rescue her son.

But she was too late.

Bertie was already on the train, trundling

through the darkness, with squeaking and moaning and groaning and roaring going on all around him and skeletons screeching and witches stirring cauldrons and coffins opening and webby sticky things touching his face and monsters grabbing at him and hot and cold winds blowing him and ... suddenly he was out in the light again.

"Bertie. Poor wee Bertie!" Mrs Boggin cried, running towards him.

"Ooooh, Mum! It was super, Mum!" said Bertie, bouncing out of the train carriage. "Ooooh, Mum. It was horrible!"

"Horrible?" said Mrs Boggin.

"Super awful horrible!" said Bertie happily.

"Oh," said Mrs Boggin. "But weren't you ... weren't you frightened of the ghosts?"

"Ghosts?" said Bertie. "I'm not

frightened of ghosts!"

And then he remembered, and turned back.

The Ghost was still sitting in the Ghost Train carriage, looking very pale and frightened, with his eyes tight shut.

"Ghost?" said Bertie gently. "Ghost? It's all right now, Ghost. The ride is over. You can open your eyes."

The Ghost opened one eye, carefully, and looked around him for monsters or skeletons or witches or horrible webby things. The only horrible thing he saw was Max, who was still green and small-monster-looking after being sick, and so the Ghost opened the other eye, shook himself, and climbed shakily out of the carriage.

"They weren't real, Ghost," said Bertie anxiously. "Not really real. Did you like the

Big Serpent? It was awful, wasn't it?"

"I enjoyed it all very much, Bertie," said the Ghost, in a muffled voice.

"And the Giant Spider! It was all oozy green, like in Monster Maze, and it went Grrrr…"

The Ghost flinched.

"I didn't actually *see* the Giant Spider, Bertie," he said at last.

"Didn't you?" said Bertie. "I did. And the monsters. I like the monsters best. They were all black and scary and…"

But the Ghost had shuffled off.

"Come on, Bertie," said Mrs Boggin. "You can tell Dad all about it when we get to the car."

And Bertie did tell Mr Boggin about it, most of the way home, while the Ghost sat silently in the luggage compartment, munching the last of the picnic sausages he had borrowed from Max, and trying to forget how frightened he had been.

"Bertie," said Mrs Boggin, when she was putting him to bed after washing all the sand and candyfloss and ice cream off him. "Bertie, did you *really* like the Ghost Train?"

"Oh yes, Mum."

"You know, Bertie," said Mrs Boggin, carefully. "I didn't like ghost trains when I was young. I used to be very scared. And do you know what I did?"

"No, Mum," said Bertie, who thought it was all a bit silly and wanted to get to sleep.

"Well, Bertie, I'll tell you. I shut my eyes tight when I was inside, and then when I came out, I pretended I had been brave, and I'd seen all the awful monsters and ghosts and not minded a bit."

"Why?"

"I didn't want people to know I was scared of monsters and ghosts and things like that, you see?" said Mrs Boggin helpfully. "But I was, really."

"I'm not."

"Aren't you? Not the tiniest bit, Bertie?"

"Of course not, Mum," said Bertie scornfully.

"I know you're not scared of *your* Ghost, Bertie," said Mrs Boggin. "But I thought you might be just a bit scared of the ones on the train."

"They're not *real*, Mum. Don't you know that?"

"Yes, yes, I know that, Bertie," said Mrs Boggin.

"They're *really* not real," said Bertie.

85

"You don't have to worry about them. Next time…" and he brightened up at the thought that there would be a next time, "next time we go to the seaside, I'll take you with me on the Ghost Train, and then you needn't be scared, not ever again."

"Thank you, Bertie," said Mrs Boggin, and she switched off the light and went downstairs.

*Then he borrowed Bertie's brush and
rewrote his coal-dust Notice.*

GHOST PAINT

"I am on holiday," said Mr Boggin cheerfully. "Nothing to do for two whole weeks."

"Oh yes there is, Jack," said Mrs Boggin, and she gave him a list of jobs.

Mr Boggin didn't look pleased. He retreated behind his *Belfast Telegraph* muttering about Holidays-Only-Coming-Once-A-Year.

"And *some* of us," said Mrs Boggin darkly, "don't get any holidays at all!"

With that parting shot she retreated into

the kitchen to eat chocolates, while Max and Elsie did the dishes and complained.

"Never get married, Bertie," said Mr Boggin, putting down his newspaper.

"Why not?" said Bertie.

Mr Boggin thought about it. "All right, Bertie," he said. "You get married, if you must."

"I'll wait until I'm grown up," said Bertie.

"Very wise," said Mr Boggin, and he went back to his newspaper.

The next morning when Bertie was sitting in the coalshed talking to the Ghost, they heard a peculiar noise coming from the yard.

SLURP. SLURP.

It started off as a slow noise, and then it got faster and faster.

SLURP. SLURP, SLURP. SLURP, SLURP,

SLURP.

SLURPSLURPSLURPSLURPSLURP.

S-L-U-R-P.

Bertie opened the door of the coalshed and looked out. He saw Mr Boggin in the yard, bending over a bucket full of white paint, which he was mixing with a stick. SLURP, SLURP, SLURP, went the paint, as Mr Boggin stirred it.

"*We* are going to paint the yard," said Max, in a proud voice. He was standing beside Mr Boggin, dressed in painting clothes, and holding a large paintbrush.

"I am painting," said Elsie. "Me, and Max, and Dad. Nobody else. And that means *not* you, Bertie."

"Bertie, you'd better go into the house out of harm's way," said Mr Boggin hurriedly, because he could see from the look on

Bertie's face that there was about to be an argument.

"So much for civilized conversation," said the Ghost, hurriedly taking down his picture of Florence Nightingale from the wall, in case someone painted over her by mistake. "Ghosts came to live here expecting peace and tranquillity, especially on a Monday morning."

"Why especially on a *Monday* morning?" Bertie asked.

"Because today is Monday," said the Ghost, putting Florence Nightingale under his arm and removing his billy-can and tea-box from the shelf. "I can see it is going to be one of those *awful* Monday mornings too."

And with that the Ghost disappeared, Florence, tea-box and all, leaving only a slight shimmer in the coalshed to show where he had been.

"Come back, Ghost," wailed Bertie.

"Get into the house, Bertie," said Mr Boggin, who didn't want to paint the yard anyway, and wasn't prepared to waste time with little boys.

Bertie went into the house.

"I want to paint," he told his mother.

"Well, you can't," she said firmly. Then she thought she would say something to please him. "Why don't you ... why don't you play with your Ghost?" she said brightly.

"Because he's gone," said Bertie, in a tragic voice.

"Gone?" said Mrs Boggin.

"Because Dad was going to paint Florence Nightingale."

"I see," said Mrs Boggin, who didn't see at all.

"So I've no one to play with, and I want to paint."

"There are only three brushes, Bertie," said Mrs Boggin patiently. "You would get covered in paint. Look at Elsie and Max and your father. They had to dress up specially. You can stay in the house and watch through the window. Won't that be fun?"

"No," said Bertie, and he went to sit in Bat-Boggin's cave under the stairs.

Bertie wanted to paint.

He could have dressed up like Max and Elsie. He could have worn the dressing-up jumper and Max's goal-keeping gloves and his father's old golf hat. All he needed was a paintbrush. Then he remembered the paintbox his Aunt Amanda Boggin had sent him from Ballynahinch as an after-measles present. The paintbox had a paintbrush in it.

It was a small paintbrush, he had to admit that. But it was a paintbrush. A small paintbrush would do for small paintings, and Bertie wasn't very big for a P2, so that all his painting had to be small, because he couldn't reach far.

With his painting clothes on and his paintbrush in his hand Bertie went downstairs ready to paint.

"Your brush is too small, and so are you, Bertie," said Mrs Boggin. "No painting."

Bertie was very cross. He went upstairs to punch Max's zobo monster, but on the way up he heard a familiar ghostly grumbling coming from the bathroom.

"G-R-U-M-B-L-E," grumbled the Ghost.

Bertie looked around the bathroom door, trying to think of something cheerful to say, because he didn't want the Ghost to disappear again.

Florence Nightingale was hanging from the towel rail.

The Ghost was standing up in the bath, scrubbing himself hard.

"Oh Ghost!" exclaimed Bertie, in alarm. "You're ... you're ... I *mean* ... you've gone all *white*. Are you ill? If you are ill, I can be the doctor. I know all about being the doctor. Doctor Gibson said I was a good one when I heard his heart. I used his stethoscope. He said I was a good doctor because..."

"That will not be necessary, Bertie," said the Ghost hastily. "It will not be necessary because I have not gone white. Ghosts are always a *little* white, semi-transparent, if you like. If I am whiter than usual, it is because I have been *painted* white."

"Oh," said Bertie.

"I was standing by the wall beneath my Notice when your brother Max painted me, without so much as a by-your-leave. I only succeeded in saving Florence by the skin of my ghostly teeth."

"Max didn't mean to paint you," said Bertie. "He couldn't see you or Florence, could he?"

"I knew it was going to be one of those Monday mornings," said the Ghost, going back to his scrubbing. "I could feel it in my bones, as soon as I got up."

"You haven't got any bones," Bertie pointed out, but the Ghost didn't think it was funny. In fact, the Ghost was getting more and more irritable with every scrub.

"Painting people. Just sloshing it on. All over me. All over my Notice. How would you like your tea-box and your billy-can painted white? Young people today have no consideration."

Bertie went away. It wasn't his fault that Max had mistaken the Ghost for the coalshed wall and painted him. It wasn't really anybody's fault, because Max couldn't see the Ghost. Max couldn't see the Ghost because he didn't believe in ghosts.

"I'll have to think of something extra-special to do to cheer the Ghost up," Bertie thought, because he was still afraid that the Ghost might disappear for good, taking Florence Nightingale with him.

He thought, and thought, and thought.

Just before tea the Bogginses went out into the yard to see how the new white paint looked.

"Marvellous," said Mrs Boggin, in an admiring voice, although privately she thought that there was one Ghost-shaped bit over by the coalshed wall that needed more paint. "Congratulations, Jack, and Max, *and* Elsie!"

"And Bertie," said Bertie.

He was sitting by the coalshed doorway, wearing his special painting clothes, and dabbing at the door with his paintbrush.

"I am painting the coalshed door," he explained proudly.

"He's just putting water on!" exclaimed Elsie. "Bertie isn't really painting at all."

"Shush," said Mrs Boggin hurriedly. "Soon be time for tea. Max, Elsie, you can lay the table," and she shooed all the children into the house, except Bertie.

The Ghost came gliding down the drainpipe with his possessions under his arm. He had been watching from the bathroom window sill, keeping out of the way in case someone decided to give him a second coat of paint.

"I've painted your door red and yellow," said Bertie proudly. "I have done it *very* nicely. I've done it red and yellow to cheer you up. It is painted in ghost paint, so they can't see it, but *you* can, can't you?"

"Of course I can," said the Ghost, getting out a hammer and nails to hang up his picture. Then he borrowed Bertie's brush and rewrote his coal-dust Notice. "There," he said, standing back. And he read out the Notice aloud.

"'*Notice.*' That's the big letters at the top, Bertie. 'Beware of the Ghost.' That's the next line. '(Signed).' That means I've signed it. 'The Ghost.' That's me, of course."

They both stood looking at the Notice and the red and yellow door, admiring their handiwork. No one else could admire it, because no one else could see it.

"It is a pity that no one else can see it," said Bertie.

"Hey," shouted Max, in an angry voice. "Who let down my bicycle tyres?"

"It wasn't me," said Bertie.

The Ghost grinned but said nothing. He had been sloshed all over with white paint, and he had to do something to get his own back.

*Off went the kite, high in the sky, with the
Ghost hanging on beneath it, shedding
coal-dust from his balaclava.*

THE GHOST AND BERTIE'S BIRTHDAY

It was Bertie's birthday.

He got a new pair of pyjamas with Batman on them and a book about Florence Nightingale and bricks and a railway and...

"A guitar!" exclaimed Max. "Super, you've got a real guitar, Bertie. Here, let me have it!"

"Max!" said Mrs Boggin sharply.

"It's mine," said Bertie, holding tight.

"I prefer pianos," said Elsie, because she had just started taking lessons with Nan

Browne on the Lisburn Road.

The Ghost took one look at the guitar and got down from the birthday cake, where he had been carefully counting the candles. He had to count the candles carefully because he had appointed himself OFFICIAL-CANDLE-BLOWING-ASSISTANT at birthdays at the Bogginses, and candle-blowing took a lot out of him. He didn't want to puff one too many. But at the sight of the guitar he made for the door.

"Ghost!" said Bertie. "What's the matter, Ghost?" But the Ghost kept on going.

"Was that your Ghost, Bertie?" Mrs Boggin asked, because she thought she might have seen a shimmer of *something*, although she couldn't be certain.

"Yes," said Bertie, and then he added in a very grand voice, "of course, none of you can see him, can you?"

"There is no Ghost," said Max, and Bertie didn't argue because at that moment the doorbell rang.

It was the postman with a big flat parcel addressed:

> Master Bertie Boggin,
> 12 Livermore Street,
> Belfast,
> Northern Ireland.

In one corner, written in smaller letters, were the words:

> *Sender*
> Miss Amanda Boggin,
> Boneybefore,
> Tenpenny Lane,
> Ballynahinch,
> Co. Down,
> Northern Ireland.

"It is a present for Bertie, from Aunt Amanda in Ballynahinch," said Mrs Boggin, and she handed the parcel over to Bertie.

It was much bigger than he was.

Bertie tore the paper off, wondering what it could be.

Some bits of plywood, some string, a lot of plastic...

"It's a kite," said Mrs Boggin.

"What did she send him a kite for?" said Mr Boggin. "He's too small for a kite."

"No I'm not," said Bertie.

"I'll fly it, and Bertie can watch," said Max, feeling pleased with himself at being able to be helpful and greedy at the same time.

"*Max!*" snapped Mrs Boggin.

"We'll go out to Ormeau Park this afternoon, and everyone can try Bertie's kite," said Mr Boggin.

"And me?" said Bertie, who was holding the kite behind his back so that Max couldn't get it.

"Of course, Bertie," said Mrs Boggin. "It is your birthday kite, isn't it?"

"Yes," said Bertie. "It is."

Bertie went out to the coalshed to tell the Ghost about the kite-flying.

There was no sign of the Ghost in the coalshed, and Florence Nightingale's face was turned towards the wall. The Ghost wasn't up the drainpipe either, although he sometimes hid there in emergencies.

"Ghost?" called Bertie, lying on his back and peering up the pipe, just to make sure.

The coal-bucket was turned upside down on the ground. It moved slightly, away from Bertie.

"Ghost?" said Bertie, getting back to his feet. "Are you under the coal-bucket?"

"No," said the coal-bucket, in a very ghost-like voice.

Bertie lifted up the coal-bucket.

The Ghost was crouching there, with his fingers in his ears.

"Ghost?" said Bertie.

"Go away," said the Ghost. "Ghosts do not like guitars. Ghosts have had to put up with lots of guitars in Haunted Cellar Discos. There are times when ghosts can't hear themselves clank for guitar noises. Go away."

"You can come out. I'm not playing my guitar. I just want to show you my kite," said Bertie.

"What kite?" said the Ghost.

"Aunt Amanda has sent me a kite," said

Bertie, displaying it. "We are all going to Ormeau Park this afternoon to fly it."

"Indeed," said the Ghost, who was still annoyed about guitars getting in everywhere.

"I shall fly the kite high, high, HIGH!" said Bertie. "I bet I fly it higher than almost anybody."

"You must think I came up the River Lagan on a bubble," said the Ghost scornfully. "You know that Max will do all the flying. He'll say you are too small, and you'll be lucky to get a turn."

"But that isn't fair," said Bertie. "It … it's … not *fair*," he stuttered, and stopped. Bertie wanted to fly his kite *himself*. It wouldn't be fair if Max did all the flying.

Bertie looked so sad that the Ghost felt sorry for what he had said.

"I tell you what, Bertie," he said quickly. "I will come with you to the park. I'll make sure you get a turn."

"Thanks," said Bertie doubtfully.

"Do we have to take little Bertie kite-flying?" Max said, when they were getting ready to go to the park. "I'll fly the kite much better without him. He's much too small."

"All the Bogginses are going," said Mr Boggin, firmly. "It is Bertie's kite, remember. Bertie has to come. If you don't like it, Max, *you* can stay at home." But he didn't say whether he would let Bertie fly the kite.

They set off to Ormeau Park.

The Ghost came too.

He was wearing his best coat and boots and a brand new balaclava helmet which he had knitted himself, in between his business trips to the Spectre's Arms. The balaclava helmet had started off white, but it ended up black because he got coal-dust on the wool. The Ghost had decided to wear it in honour of Bertie's birthday, and because it was a very blowy day.

"I will fly the kite first," said Mr Boggin. "Just to show you all how to do it."

"Then me," said Max. "Bertie is too small to hold on to the string. He would let go. So it must be me, mustn't it?"

No sooner had he said it than *something* breathed very cold air down the back of his neck.

"Ouch!" said Max. "What was that?"

"Me," said the Ghost, but no one heard him except Bertie.

Up went the kite, high in the air, and off went Mr Boggin running across the park.

It was good kite-flying weather, very windy, and the Ghost retired to the shade of a tree to read Bertie's birthday book on Florence Nightingale, which Bertie had very kindly lent him.

The kite-flying went on and on.

"When is it your turn?" the Ghost asked, when he got tired of reading.

"I don't think I'm getting one," said Bertie. "Max says I'm too small. And maybe I am," he added dolefully. "The wind does blow the kite about a lot, doesn't it?"

"Your kite won't blow away," said the Ghost. "If you get a turn, I will help you to hold on to it."

"Thank you," said Bertie.

"Dad," said Max. "Can one of us have a turn?"

"In a minute, Max," said Mr Boggin, and

off he dashed again.

"*Dad*," said Max.

Mr Boggin looked annoyed.

"You *promised* we could have a turn, Dad," said Max.

Mr Boggin didn't like being interrupted in his kite-flying, and he made up his mind there and then that Max would have to wait.

"It is Bertie's kite," Mr Boggin announced. "Bertie must fly it."

"Let's go home," said Elsie, who didn't like kites.

"Bertie's too small," said Max.

"Who wants to fly a stupid kite anyway?" said Elsie, whose big nose was getting cold.

"Now, Bertie," said Mr Boggin. "I am going to let you hold on to the string, just for a moment."

Bertie looked at the kite, high above him,

dipping and whipping in the wind. There was a lot of wind.

"I will help you to hold it, Bertie," said the Ghost helpfully. "We'll both hold on."

Bertie took hold of the kite string, and Mr Boggin let go.

"Ooooh! Help!" cried Bertie. The wind blew, and the kite dragged him forward and then ...

... poor Bertie twisted ...

... and tripped ...

... and fell flat on his face ...

... and let the kite go!

Off went the kite, high in the sky, with the Ghost hanging on beneath it, shedding coal-dust from his balaclava.

"Ha ha ha," laughed Max. "I told you Bertie was too titchy."

Mr Boggin wiped Bertie's nose

114

automatically and told him not to worry. Then he said a few short sharp words to Max on the vexed subject of being nice to little brothers, and they all went home.

Kite-less.

"My kite blew away," Bertie told Mrs Boggin, when they got back to Livermore Street.

"And he's lost his Florence Nightingale book," said Elsie meanly. "He took it with him, but he hasn't brought it back."

"Poor Bertie," said Mrs Boggin.

Bertie went sadly out to the coalshed.

It was empty.

The Ghost was blowing about Belfast, somewhere, and would keep on blowing about until the wind died down. Perhaps he would never come back.

"He will come back," sniffed Bertie.

"I want him to come back," said Bertie.

He sat in the empty coalshed and waited, but the Ghost did not return.

"Bertie?" said Mrs Boggin, putting her head around the door. She was going to scold him when she saw him sitting on the coal, but poor Bertie looked so sad that she decided not to. After all, it was his birthday, and he had lost his kite.

"Birthday tea for Bertie!" Mr Boggin announced, handing out the paper hats.

Bertie put on a long flat one, that drooped over his face.

He spilt his orange juice over his new blue trousers.

He didn't feel like little sausages on sticks, the ice cream was too cold for him, and the jelly cats and dogs were the wrong colour.

"I'll eat yours, Bertie," said Max.

"Max," said Mrs Boggin, in a warning voice.

"Max can have them, Mum," said Bertie.

He brightened up a bit when it came to blowing out the candles on his birthday cake, and took a big breath to make sure that they all went out first blow, so that his wish would come true. He took a long time about wishing, because he had to wish very hard if he was going to get his Ghost back.

"Happy birthday dear Bertie," everyone sang, but it wasn't.

"I think I'll just go to bed, if nobody minds," said Bertie, half an hour before his ordinary time, and he went off up the stairs.

"Oh dear," said Mrs Boggin, but then she had to attend to Max, who was being sick from eating too many jelly cats and dogs, and it was almost half an hour before she went upstairs to Bertie's room.

"Bertie?" she said, putting her head round the door.

Bertie wasn't there.

She looked in Max's room, and the bathroom, and then she went to the front of the house, and looked in her own bedroom.

Bertie was standing at the window, looking down the street.

Coming up the street ...

... was

    ... a

      ... KITE!

That was what Mrs Boggin saw, looking over Bertie's shoulder. It was moving steadily up the middle of the street, heading straight for Bertie's house. It was flapping loosely on the end of its string, which just at that moment gave a sort of hop, and tied itself neatly to the railings outside the Bogginses' front door.

"I... I..." Mrs Boggin stammered, in amazement. She knew kites couldn't fly themselves.

"He brought it back," said Bertie, smiling all over his face. "The Ghost brought my kite back, Mum!"

And he bounced off downstairs to collect it, despite the fact that he had no trousers on.

Mrs Boggin sat down on the end of the bed.

Then she got up.

Then she sat down again.

"Happy birthday, Bertie," said the Ghost, gliding towards the coalshed, clutching the piece of cake Bertie had saved for him.

Bertie went upstairs to celebrate with his kite and Mrs Boggin came downstairs to

119

have a serious talk with Mr Boggin about kites that fly themselves home.

"Stuff and nonsense, Edna," said Mr Boggin. "I expect some of the neighbours brought it back."

"But I saw it, Jack! I saw it coming up the middle of the street."

"I think you should lie down for a little, dear," said Mr Boggin, and she did.

"Ghosts are good at finding blackberries,"
explained the Ghost, in a contented voice.

THE GHOST GOES BLACKBERRYING

One morning when the Ghost came out of the coalshed to do his morning exercises, he found Bertie standing by the yard tap looking important.

"Good morning, Bertie," said the Ghost, who was usually polite. Having said "Good morning" the Ghost went on with what he had come out to do, for he did not like having his daily routine disturbed. Ghosts are creatures of habit.

The Ghost stood still, took a deep breath,

and started to jump up and down, flapping his ghostly arms.

"Hup! Yup! Hup! Yup! Hup! Yup! Hup!"

"This is my jar," said Bertie importantly, holding out a large coffee jar with a piece of string tied around the top to make a handle.

"Hup! Yup! Hup! Yup! Hup! Yup! Hup! Yup!" The Ghost was so busy with his exercises that he had no time to pay attention to Bertie.

"Max has a jar, and so has Elsie," said Bertie. "We are all going blackberrying. We are going to fill up our jars with scrumptious blackberries!"

"Yup! Hup! Yup! Hup! Yup! Hup! Yup! Hup!" went the Ghost, regardless, but on the last "Hup!" he tripped over his spectral feet and sat down very hard on the ground.

"Oh dear!" gasped the Ghost. With all his

jumping up and down he had become more transparent than usual, and he was out of breath.

"Are you all right, Ghost?" Bertie asked anxiously.

"Oh dear," panted the Ghost. "Oh dear, water."

Bertie quickly got him a drink of water from the yard tap, using the Ghost's billy-can for the purpose.

"I'm afraid that this Ghost isn't what he used to be," admitted the Ghost, leaning back against the drainpipe.

"What used you to be?" Bertie asked.

"Don't ask cheeky questions," said the Ghost in a huffy voice. "Ghosts are old and important. They are entitled to respect and privacy in their old age."

"I'm very sorry," said Bertie.

The Ghost stood up. "I don't feel up to blackberrying this morning," he said thoughtfully. "I think I will go back to my coalshed and put my feet up on the slack with yesterday's *Evening Haunt*, if you don't mind."

"I do mind," said Bertie. "I want you to get some good fresh air. I won't enjoy myself unless you come too. You can sit in the back of the Mini and I will bring you lots of blackberries. Then you won't get too tired, will you?"

The Ghost looked doubtful about it.

"*Please*, Ghost?" said Bertie.

"Thank you very much for suggesting it, Bertie," said the Ghost wearily. "I shall be delighted to accept your kind offer." He didn't *sound* delighted, but Bertie didn't notice that.

The Bogginses set off in the Mini complete with Tojo and the Ghost, who were now very friendly.

"That dog is mad," said Mr Boggin. "Look at him jumping around licking the luggage space. Sit down, Tojo!"

Tojo sat, and then got up again quickly, because he had sat on the Ghost, who was already beginning to regret his decision to come.

"What's wrong with him now?" said Mr Boggin impatiently.

"It's my Ghost," said Bertie, in a small voice, but Mr Boggin didn't hear him.

Elsie did.

"Bertie's Ghost," she giggled. "Tojo sat on Bertie's Ghost!"

At that moment someone tipped Elsie's school beret over her eyes.

"Who did that?" she demanded, pushing it back.

"*Children!*" said Mrs Boggin, in a puzzled voice. "No more of that, or we'll stop the car." She had seen the beret slip slowly forward over Elsie's eyes and nose, as if someone in the luggage space had pushed it.

"*But I don't believe in ghosts,*" she reminded herself.

"Bags I those bushes!" said Max, springing out of the car when they stopped in Hunter's Lane.

"These are mine!" said Elsie, leaping over the ditch to get at them.

The Ghost staggered out of the car, vowing that he would never travel in the luggage space with Tojo again. He liked Tojo, but he *dis*liked being sat upon.

The blackberries on Max's bush were fat

and soft and sweet when he tasted them. Elsie's were gorgeous too.

"One for me, one for my jar," said Elsie, popping three blackberries into her mouth, and one into her jar. She couldn't be bothered to keep an *exact* count, and she liked eating blackberries.

"Here you are, Bertie," said Mr Boggin. "Have some of mine. Would you like me to lift you over the ditch so that you can reach some?"

The trouble was that all the best blackberries were high up. Bertie could have crossed the ditch himself, but he didn't like getting close to the brambles, and the only blackberries he could reach without crossing the ditch were small, hard, red and green ones, which didn't taste sweet.

"I don't like brambles," said Bertie, and

he took a handful of Mr Boggin's blackberries and headed back to the car to give some to the Ghost.

Of course, when he reached the car, he found that the Ghost had gone.

"Ghost?" said Bertie, looking up and down the lane.

"I've lost my Ghost," he told Mrs Boggin.

"Yes, dear," said Mrs Boggin. She had snagged her tights on a bramble and wasn't really paying attention to him. "That's nice."

It wasn't nice. Bertie was worried. He went up the lane and looked beneath the car and up the exhaust pipe, just in case. He looked behind the bushes and then as he approached the gate of Mr Hunter's house he heard a familiar voice talking about Florence Nightingale.

"Ghost!" cried Bertie, climbing over

the gate.

The Ghost and Tojo were sitting in the tall grass. The Ghost was eating specially selected blackberries from a pile inside his hat, which was upside down on the ground beside him. Tojo was wagging his tail, and keeping well clear of the Ghost, who had delivered a short lecture on not sitting upon ghosts you can't see.

"Ghosts are good at finding blackberries," explained the Ghost, in a contented voice. "Ghosts know all the best places to look."

"Could you show me some?" asked Bertie.

"Max! Elsie! Bertie! Tojo!" called Mr Boggin. "Come on! Time to go home."

"Max, your jar is only half full," said Mrs

131

Boggin. "And Elsie's is no better. You've eaten most of them, you greedy lot. Now there will be no blackberries to take home, and no bramble jelly."

"Oh yes there will," said Bertie.

Bertie's jar was brimful, and so was Bertie. Bertie's blackberries were bigger, juicier and riper than anyone else's, because they came from the Ghost's Special Place in Mr Hunter's field.

"Well done, Bertie," exclaimed Mrs Boggin. "You are the best blackberry-getter in the house."

"Not *quite* the best," muttered the Ghost, but as nobody could hear him but Bertie and as Bertie wasn't listening, it didn't matter.

*The Ghost perched on Bertie's window sill, with
the turnip-head lantern glowing beside him.*

A GHOSTLY HALLOWE'EN

Bertie was very excited.

"It's Hallowe'en! It's Hallowe'en!" he hummed to himself, bouncing out into the back yard, and almost falling over Tojo, who was guarding his friend's coalshed.

"Hullo, Ghost," said Bertie, putting his head around the door.

"Humph! 'Lo," said the Ghost, over his shoulder. He was looking very red in his pale face, and altogether flustered.

Bertie was surprised to see the Ghost up and about so early. He had expected to find him sitting down having a quiet worry, or catching up on the *Evening Haunt* with his feet up on the slack. Instead, the Ghost was no more than a transparent blur as he wisped around the coalshed.

"What are you doing, Ghost?" Bertie asked.

"I am very busy, Bertie," said the Ghost. "Please do not interrupt me. I have a lot to do." And he started muttering and counting on his wispy fingers.

"The Bogginses are having a special Hallowe'en Party," Bertie announced. "There will be ducking for apples and sparklers and fireworks and turnip-head lanterns and a pumpkin head and cracking nuts in the fire and telling fortunes and lots and lots of special witch food."

"Very nice," said the Ghost. "Very nice

indeed, for those who have time for it. Would you mind moving over? You are standing on my haunting cloak."

"Oh," said Bertie, sounding disappointed. "I thought you would be pleased. I thought you would want to hear all about our party. I was going to tell you lots of things. You *usually* like parties."

"Bertie," the Ghost said, interrupting before his Best Friend could get started on the subject of parties. "Bertie, it is *Hallowe'en*."

"I know," said Bertie. "Ice cream with Magic Dust, and paper hats and nuts and turnip heads and bonfires and..."

"Not for ghosts, Bertie," said the Ghost, shaking his head. "Ghosts are kept very busy at Hallowe'en. It isn't just the Spectre's Arms, you know! I could manage that. I've so many special Hallowe'en haunting engagements that I don't know where to begin. I'll be glad when Hallowe'en is over, I can tell you. I won't budge out of my coalhole for a week."

"I see," said Bertie, beginning to understand.

"It wouldn't be so bad if we got overtime," said the Ghost bitterly.

"I suppose not," said Bertie, who wasn't sure what overtime was. Then he cheered up. "You will come to our Hallowe'en Party, won't you? You know how much you love parties."

The Ghost loved parties. At birthdays he helped with the candle-blowing and jelly-eating, and he liked squeakers and paper hats and games, except when people trod on him playing them. The Ghost often got over-excited at parties, and usually had to rest in the coalshed for days afterwards with only Florence Nightingale to keep him company.

"You will come, won't you?" said Bertie.

"I wish I could, Bertie," said the Ghost. "There is nothing I would like better. But I can't. My Haunting Book is filled up with appointments. By the time I get home, your party will be over."

"That isn't fair," said Bertie, and he went in to tell his mother about it.

"Well now, Bertie," said Mrs Boggin. "Hallowe'en is a special Ghosty time. I am not at all surprised that your Ghost has a lot to do."

"But he is such a kind Ghost, and he's my Best Friend. I want him at our party. He's always so happy at parties. I won't like our party one bit if the Ghost has to miss it."

139

And Bertie looked glum.

"I'm afraid there isn't much I can do about it," said Mrs Boggin. "But I'll try to think of something, that's a promise."

It was a good party.

It was a *very* good party.

There were sparklers and fireworks and turnip-head lanterns and ice cream with Magic Dust and a big yellow pumpkin and cracking nuts in front of the fire and ducking for apples and telling fortunes and small sausages on sticks and ham sandwiches and chocolate eyes and lots and lots of food for Bertie and Max and Elsie and all their friends, even Tojo, who got a special slice of Hallowe'en cake in his dish and almost choked on the five pence piece hidden in it. There was a dark cave in the box-room with a witch in a black cloak and green hat. The witch gave away sweeties, speaking in a voice that sounded astoundingly like Aunt Amanda Boggin's.

"But it can't be Aunt Amanda," Max said. "She is in Ballynahinch."

"It must have been a real witch!" said Bertie.

Bertie played and ate until it was time to go to bed.

He put on his pyjamas and got into bed, and his mother came to switch off the light.

"Did you enjoy the party, Bertie?" she asked hopefully.

"Yes," said Bertie. "It was trillions and billions, that's what it was. But the Ghost couldn't come. I didn't enjoy that."

"No," said Mrs Boggin. "I'm very sorry about the Ghost, Bertie."

"I expect he is still out haunting," said Bertie.

"Well," said Mrs Boggin carefully, "you know, I *thought* I saw him during the apple-ducking. Perhaps he managed to look in, just for a minute."

"You didn't see him," said Bertie firmly. "I am the only one who can see him, and I *know* he wasn't there. It isn't fair that he had to spend all night haunting, even if it is Hallowe'en. The Ghost loves parties."

"I agree," said Mrs Boggin.

"You promised you would think of something," said Bertie.

"I promised to *try* to think of something," Mrs Boggin said. "And I... WAIT! Wait! I have an idea! Put on your dressing-gown and slippers and come downstairs with me this minute, Bertie Boggin."

"Why is Bertie going downstairs?" said Elsie, who was trying to comb toffee out of her hair in the bathroom. The toffee had got into her hair when Max threw it at Tojo.

"Bertie and I have a Secret Mission," said Mrs Boggin importantly.

"Now, Bertie," she said, when they got down to the kitchen. "Get me my plastic container from the cupboard."

Bertie got the container.

"Right," said Mrs Boggin. "In goes one paper hat, one cracker, one squeaker, one slice of apple tart, six nuts…"

"And the nut-crackers," said Bertie. "He'll need the nut-crackers."

"Nut-crackers," said Mrs Boggin, adding them. "*Now*… Coalshed, here we come!"

"Oh for goodness sake, Edna!" muttered Mr Boggin.

"I'll bring my turnip-head lantern," said Bertie. "But there are no more sparklers."

"I don't suppose the Ghost will miss them," said Mrs Boggin. "There we are! A whole Hallowe'en Party for the Ghost. We'll leave it out for him when he comes back from his haunting."

"Smashing!" said Bertie.

Bertie went to bed, and almost to sleep.

Maybe he *did* go to sleep. It was a long time afterwards when he heard: "Squeeaaakk! Squeeeaaak! Squeeeaaaaakk!" coming from the yard beneath his window.

"Ghost?" Bertie called, and the Ghost came gliding up the drainpipe and perched on Bertie's window sill, with the turnip-head lantern glowing beside him. The Ghost was wearing his paper hat, and cracking nuts in between squeaking his squeaker.

144

"I'm having a lovely party, Bertie," he said. "Thank you for inviting me."

"And thank you for coming," said Bertie.

"Squeaaaak! Squeeaaaaaak!" went the Ghost, blowing on his squeaker. In the room below, Mrs Boggin stirred uneasily in her sleep, but Mr Boggin didn't hear a thing.

*And there, shimmering in the glow of the
Christmas tree lights, fast asleep in the
best armchair ... was the Ghost.*

A HAPPY CHRISTMAS
FOR THE GHOST

It was Christmas Eve, and the Ghost was busy decorating the coalshed. He had strung red and yellow streamers round the walls, and poked holly through the holes in the tin roof. A piece of mistletoe dangled in the doorway and Florence Nightingale's frame was draped with silver tinsel. In the far corner there glowed a ghostly Christmas tree, all red and green and gold and shiny.

"Oooooooooo! Ghost!" said Bertie, looking at it with saucer eyes. He thought it

147

was the best Christmas tree he had ever seen.

The Ghost sat down rather unsteadily on the slack, resting his glass on the coal-bucket beside him. The Ghost had just come back from the Spectre's Arms, where he had been having a small extra Festive Haunt, with breaks for refreshments.

"It is time you were in bed, Bertie," said the Ghost. "Santa Claus will soon be here."

"Max says that there is no Santa Claus," said Bertie.

"Max says there are no ghosts," said the Ghost. "But Max doesn't know everything, does he? Ghosts are rather like Santa Claus."

"Are they?" said Bertie.

"Oh yes, they are," said the Ghost. "I'm a ghost, and you believe in me, so you can see me. Max doesn't believe in me, and he can't see me. It is the same with Santa Claus, but

148

more important, because if nobody believed in Santa Claus, there would be no Christmas. I feel sorry for Max."

"So do I," said Bertie, and he went off upstairs to bed.

"Mum," said Bertie, as Mrs Boggin was tucking him in. "Mum, I'm sorry for Max, because Max doesn't believe in Santa Claus."

"Doesn't he?" said Mrs Boggin.

"Mum," said Bertie. "Do *you* believe in Santa Claus?"

"Of course I do, wee Bertie," said Mrs Boggin. "You wait until the morning, and you'll see."

"But you don't believe in ghosts, do you?" said Bertie. "You don't believe in *my* Ghost."

Mrs Boggin took a long time replying. "I don't know, Bertie," she said, in the end.

149

"I don't know what to think about your Ghost. Sometimes I … but it doesn't really matter what I believe, does it? So long as *you* believe in him."

"That's right," said Bertie. "My Ghost will still be there, so long as I believe in him." And he cuddled down beneath the sheets to go to sleep.

But he didn't go to sleep.

Bertie lay in bed hoping and hoping for a red and yellow tricycle like the one in Mrs Boggin's big catalogue.

"Tricycles cost a lot of money, Bertie," Mrs Boggin had told him. "But we'll see at Christmas time."

Now it was Christmas, almost.

"TRICYCLE."

"TRICYCLE."

Bertie concentrated very hard, in the hope

150

that believing in tricycles would make one come.

The Ghost came floating into the room and perched on the end of Bertie's bed. He waved at Bertie.

"Just doing my rounds," he said. "I've got to make sure all the stockings are up."

"Mine is one of Dad's," said Bertie, who had picked the biggest sock he could find. Then he asked the Ghost a question.

"Ghost," Bertie said, "if Max doesn't believe in Santa Claus, what will happen to *his* Christmas stocking? You said that there would be no Christmas if people didn't believe in Santa Claus, and Max doesn't."

The Ghost looked serious. "Then you'll have to do his believing for him, Bertie," he said.

"Oh," said Bertie. "Do you think I could?"

"I'm sure you could," said the Ghost.

"I believe in Santa Claus," said Bertie.

"Oh, I know you do," said the Ghost. "Good night, Bertie," and he glided off in the general direction of the Spectre's Arms and the Haunted Cellar Disco, where his presence was urgently required.

"Tricycle," thought Bertie, thinking very hard, and "I believe in Santa Claus for me *and* Max," and "TRICYCLE," again, and again, and again, because the tricycle was very important.

"TRICYCLE!!!"

He went to sleep.

"Hip-yip hurrah! It's Christmas!" Max was dancing on the stairs. In one hand he waved a telescope, and in the other his half-empty Christmas stocking. He was eating mandarin oranges and chocolate at the same time, with a spud gun sticking out of the belt of his pyjamas.

Elsie said "Oooooh," and "Aaaaaah!" and started eating too, whilst she sorted out the lovely things in her stocking. There was a blue scarf and a diary and a pen and a talking doll.

"Toooole-uuuu! Ouuutle-oooo!" went Bertie, on the gold trumpet he had pulled from his stocking. "Tooole-utttle-utttttle!"

"Children, it is only six o'clock," muttered a bleary-eyed Mr Boggin.

"Hip-yip! Ooooooo-aaah! Toootle-uuttttle-uttle!" went all the Bogginses in chorus, as they headed down the stairs.

The door of the Christmas Room was shut.

The Ghost bounced up and down on the

153

hall-stand, wearing his haunting hat and his pyjamas and eating chocolate doubloons from his stocking.

"Wait till you *see*! Wait till you *see* what's in there, Bertie!" he whispered.

"Now," said Mrs Boggin, opening the door of the Christmas Room. "One child at a time. Bertie first, because he is the smallest."

Bertie went into the Christmas Room.

The curtains were pulled tight, the pile of presents was lit by the glint of the Christmas tree lights.

There were fat parcels and thin parcels, big parcels and little parcels and tiny parcels, and green parcels and red parcels and gold parcels and yellow parcels, and parcels that looked like bottles and parcels that didn't, and a thing like a swingball for Max and a *huge* painting-set for Elsie (complete with easel) and …

… glittering in the darkness …

… red and yellow, with a shiny bright bell…

"Tricycle," breathed Bertie. "My TRICYCLE!"

He touched it.

He rang the bell.

It was *real*.

It *really* was.

Everyone had a very happy Christmas at Number 12 Livermore Street.

"You only got that telescope from Santa Claus because of me," Bertie told Max, and Max didn't even thump him.

"You've all eaten too much!" said Mrs Boggin.

"Good," said Mr Boggin, and the rest of the Bogginses agreed with him. All except Tojo, that is, for he was still too busily engaged in eating the biggest-bone-in-the-world (given to him by Max, and tied up with a blue ribbon by Elsie) to agree with anything.

"Time for bed," said Mrs Boggin, at last.

They went to bed.

"Mum," said Bertie, as she was tucking him in, "the Ghost said I was to thank you very much for having him."

"You can tell him it's a pleasure, Bertie," said Mrs Boggin. And then she added: "If I see him, I'll tell him so myself."

"You can't see him, Mum," said Bertie. "You can't see the Ghost if you don't believe in him."

"Y-e-s," said Mrs Boggin. "Well … you see … Bertie, I think I…"

"Mum," said Max. "I think I've got a sick tummy."

Mrs Boggin went to deal with Max's tummy. Then she had to rush downstairs to fetch Bertie's book about spiders, which Aunt Amanda had sent him from Ballynahinch. Elsie couldn't sleep, and wanted to get up and watch the late film. Then Mr Boggin couldn't find his slippers.

Mrs Boggin was run off her feet looking after them all.

"Bed," said Mr Boggin, who had had a very hard day sitting down.

Mrs Boggin let Tojo out and in again, stoked up the boiler, put out the kitchen light, stole a nip of cold ham and turkey, and went into the Christmas Room.

And there ...

... shimmering in the glow of the

Christmas tree lights …

… fast asleep in the best armchair with a large glass of Mr Boggin's Bristol Cream sherry in his hand …

… Mrs Boggin *saw* the Ghost.

She stood absolutely still, and her mouth dropped open.

"Bertie's Ghost!" she said.

"Is that you, Florence?" muttered the Ghost, still deep in his sleep. He didn't wake up, and Mrs Boggin didn't waken him. Instead she put out the light and tiptoed gently out of the room.

THE

END